BASKETBALL LEGENDS

Kareem Abdul-Jabbar
Charles Barkley
Larry Bird
Kobe Bryant
Wilt Chamberlain
Clyde Drexler
Julius Erving
Patrick Ewing
Kevin Garnett
Anfernee Hardaway
Tim Hardaway
The Head Coaches
Grant Hill
Juwan Howard
Allen Iverson
Magic Johnson
Michael Jordan
Shawn Kemp
Jason Kidd
Reggie Miller
Alonzo Mourning
Hakeem Olajuwon
Shaquille O'Neal
Gary Payton
Scottie Pippen
David Robinson
Dennis Rodman
John Stockton
Keith Van Horn
Antoine Walker
Chris Webber

CHELSEA HOUSE PUBLISHERS

DENNIS RODMAN

Steven Frank

Introduction by
Chuck Daly

CHELSEA HOUSE PUBLISHERS
Philadelphia

Produced by Daniel Bial and Associates
New York, New York

Picture research by Alan Gottlieb
Cover illustration by Bradford Brown

3 5 7 9 8 6 4 2

Library of Congress Cataloging-in-Publication Data

Frank, Steven.
    Dennis Rodman/Steven Frank.
       p. cm.—(Basketball Legends)
    Includes bibliographical references (p.) and index.
    Summary: Describes the personal life and basketball career of the
flamboyant athlete who has played with both the Detroit Pistons and the
Chicago Bulls.
    ISBN 0-7910-4388-6 (hardcover)
    1. Rodman, Dennis, 1961- —Juvenile literature. 2. Basketball players—
United States—Juvenile literature. [1. Rodman, Dennis, 1961- . 2. Basket–
ball players. 3. Afro-Americans—Biography.]
I. Title. II. Series.
GV884.R618F73   1997
796.323'092—dc21
[B]   97-14991
                                                           CIP
                                                           AC

CONTENTS

BECOMING A BASKETBALL LEGEND

Chuck Daly

What does it take to be a basketball superstar? Two of the three things it takes are easy to spot. Any great athlete must have excellent skills and tremendous dedication. The third quality needed is much harder to define, or even put in words. Others call it leadership or desire to win, but I'm not sure that explains it fully. This third quality relates to the athlete's thinking process, a certain mentality and work ethic. One can coach athletic skills, and while few superstars need outside influence to help keep them dedicated, it is possible for a coach to offer some well-timed words in order to keep that athlete fully motivated. But a coach can do no more than appeal to a player's will to win; how much that player is then capable of ensuring victory is up to his own internal workings.

In recent times, we have been fortunate to have seen some of the best to play the game. Larry Bird, Magic Johnson, and Michael Jordan had all three components of superstardom in full measure. They brought their teams to numerous championships, and made the players around them better. (They also made their coaches look smart.)

I myself coached a player who belongs in that class, Isiah Thomas, who helped lead the Detroit Pistons to consecutive NBA crowns. Isiah is not tall—he's just over six feet—but he could do whatever he wanted with the ball. And what he wanted to do most was lead and win.

All the players I mentioned above and those whom this series will chronicle are tremendously gifted athletes, but for the most part, you can't play professional basketball at all unless you have excellent skills. And few players get to stay on their team unless they are willing to dedicate themselves to improving their talents even more, learning about their opponents, and finding a way to join with their teammates and win.

It's that third element that separates the good player from the superstar, the memorable players from the legends of the game. Superstars know when to take over the game. If the situation calls for a defensive stop, the superstars stand up and do it. If the situation calls for a key pass, they make it. And if the situation calls for a big shot, they want the ball. They don't want the ball simply because of their own glory or ego. Instead they know—and their teammates know—that they are the ones who can deliver, regardless of the pressure.

The words "legend" and "superstar" are often tossed around without real meaning. Taking a hard look at some of those who truly can be classified as "legends" can provide insight into the things that brought them to that level. All of them developed their legacy over numerous seasons of play, even if certain games will always stand out in the memories of those who saw them. Those games typically featured amazing feats of all-around play. No matter how great the fans thought the superstars were, these players were capable of surprising the fans, their opponents, and occasionally even themselves. The desire to win took over, and with their dedication and athletic skills already in place, they were capable of the most astonishing achievements.

CHUCK DALY, most recently the head coach of the New Jersey Nets, guided the Detroit Pistons to two straight NBA championships, in 1989 and 1990. He earned a gold medal as coach of the 1992 U.S. Olympic basketball team—the so-called "Dream Team"—and was inducted into the Pro Basketball Hall of Fame in 1994.

1
THE WORM

On February 25, 1990, Dennis Rodman was dying for a chance to take on Patrick Ewing. Rodman's Detroit Pistons were faltering. In order to win, the Pistons would have to stop Ewing, one of the NBA's top scorers.

With five minutes left in the game, Rodman asked his coach, Chuck Daly, if he could defend the Knicks' center. Many coaches would have just laughed off the request. After all, Rodman, a forward, was 6'8" to Ewing's 7'0", and a good 50 pounds lighter. Other than Piston fans, few people had heard of Rodman—this was long before his tattoos and women's wear made him front-page material.

But Daly knew "The Worm" well. Rodman had earned the nickname as a kid for the way he wiggled and shook while playing pinball. But the name stuck when Rodman started playing basketball because it seemed to describe as well

Dennis Rodman broke into tears when he was honored with the NBA's Defensive Player of the Year Award in May 1990.

the way Rodman could use his wiry build and speed to worm his way around the court. So when Rodman asked for a crack at Ewing, Daly said sure.

The gamble paid off. In those final few minutes of the game, the Knicks kept with their typical strategy—get the ball to Ewing. But with Rodman guarding him, Ewing was kept to only two points during those last crucial minutes of the game. The Pistons won 98-87.

About two months later, Rodman and Ewing once again met: in the Eastern Conference semifinals. Whichever team won this series would move on to the Eastern Conference finals. Even though they'd won the championship the previous year, there was no guarantee the Pistons would be able to pull it off again. Before the finals, many members of the press wrote about how, during the last several games of the season, the Pistons' performance had been uneven and often sloppy. They also didn't have a star scorer like Patrick Ewing.

During the semifinals the Pistons proved that Ewing could be stopped—the way to do it was as a team. While the Knicks tended to rely on Ewing as their star player, the Pistons could work together like a well-oiled machine. The Pistons won two of the first three games. In Game 4, Ewing played only six minutes of the first half due to foul trouble. But in the second half, he came out smoking.

Rodman was recovering from a stomach virus, but he refused to give in to his illness. In the final four minutes, Daly again assigned the smaller man against the Knick star. New York continually tried to get the ball to their center, but Rodman kept Ewing in check. He kept Ewing

In 1990, the Detroit Pistons repeated as world champions. One reason they got past the Chicago Bulls was that Rodman made Michael Jordan work hard on both ends of the court.

from getting good looks at the basket, and even blocked a key shot. Ewing managed to score 30 points, but he missed far more shots than he made—just what the Pistons wanted.

With the Pistons leading 85-80, Rodman found himself with the ball and an open shot. He missed his jumper, though, and the Knicks' Mark Jackson took the rebound and raced up court. Rodman, unfazed by his miss, streaked after Jackson. If the guard scored, the Knicks would be down by only a three-point field goal.

Rodman forgot about his stomach virus, forgot about how tired he was from playing the long, tight game. Giving every ounce of energy, he surprised Jackson just as he was going for the

Rodman fights for a loose ball with Kiki Vanderweghe of the New York Knicks as Bill Laimbeer looks on during the 1990 playoffs.

layup and knocked the ball away. The Pistons got the ball back, scored, and the Knicks were unable to come close again.

Rodman finished the game with 14 points, 14 rebounds, and 2 steals. His play helped oust the Knicks and bring Detroit its next challenge—the Eastern Conference finals, against the Chicago Bulls and their star guard Michael Jordan.

In the first quarter of the first game, Jordan came out on fire. He scored 26 points in the first quarter alone. But at the end of the quarter, he headed toward the basket, and Rodman raced to join John Salley and Joe Dumars to try to cut off his angle. Jordan tried to cut across the court sideways. Rodman bumped him, sending him down onto the floor.

Jordan came down hard, bruising his upper leg. He scored just eight points in the rest of the game. The injury kept Jordan from playing his best in Game 2 as well, and Detroit won both matches.

In Games 3 and 4, the Bulls gave the Pistons a taste of their own medicine. By playing high-pressure defense on their home court, Chicago kept Detroit's scoring power in check, and tied the series. The Bulls and Pistons split the next two games. One game would decide who would go on to the championship and who would go home.

Rodman had a sprained ankle, but he didn't let it affect his playing. The combination of Isiah Thomas's shooting abilities, at a peak in this game, and their suffocating defense enabled the Pistons to take the game, 93-74, and the series. Chicago's 74 point finish was the lowest score the Bulls had during the entire playoff series— a testament to the success of the Pistons' stellar defense.

The Pistons were on their way to the NBA finals. They had a chance to go down in history as one of the few teams to win back-to-back championships.

At the start of the season, few would have said Rodman was the key to the Pistons' success. But on May 7, just before the Pistons were to start their semifinal series against the Knicks, "The Worm" was named the NBA's Defensive Player of the Year. As he stood on the podium of the Auburn Palace listening to praise from his teammates and coach, Rodman was overcome by emotion. As his eyes welled up with tears, he said, "This proves to me that people do like me, that they like the way I play."

Those who had seen how tough Rodman could be on the court might have been surprised to see him so easily moved to tears. But anyone who knew of Rodman's troubled past and the obstacles he overcame to get to the NBA understood exactly what that moment meant to him.

2
TURNAROUND

Sometimes, like on a rollercoaster, you have to go all the way to the bottom before you can start climbing up. For Rodman, it took a night in jail and several months living on the streets before he was able to get off the dead-end track his life had started on and turn everything around.

Dennis Rodman was born on May 31, 1961, in Trenton, N.J. When he was three years old, his father, Philander Rodman, suddenly stopped coming home. It would be years before Dennis would learn the reason why—that his father had been neglecting his wife and instead spending his time with other women. Tired of putting up with her husband's lack of commitment to herself and the family, Shirley decided to move away, bringing Dennis and his two sisters, Debra and Kim, to Dallas, Texas, where she was originally from.

Shirley Rodman raised three kids by herself after her husband stopped coming home when Dennis was three years old.

They moved to the Oak Cliff housing project, where they remained throughout the duration of Dennis and his sisters' childhoods. Life was not easy for Shirley and her children. Money was tight and they had few luxuries.

Still, Shirley vowed that her children would always have food, clothing, and a home where they could feel safe. Forced to raise her kids alone, Shirley did whatever it took to make certain the family survived, sometimes holding two or three jobs at a time. She always kept food on the table and clothes on their backs, but she worked such long hours she didn't have lots of time to be around her children.

Dennis was a quiet and sensitive child. He missed his father and when his mother was at work, he missed her too. A shy boy, he had trouble making friends and spent most of his time moping around the house.

As Dennis entered his teens, he also became self conscious about his body. A skinny and gawky kid, he was often teased because his younger sisters were both taller than he. The Rodman girls were also gifted athletes, starring on their high school basketball team. Dennis took pride in his sisters' success, but at the same time, their popularity couldn't help but make him feel worse about himself, like he was the family loser.

Although he lacked his sisters' confidence and natural grace, he still enjoyed playing sports for fun and would often go with his sisters to the neighborhood recreation center to hang out and get in on a game. When he reached the tenth grade, he tried out for for the football team. Although a fast runner, he was cut because he was too small. He did make the junior varsity basketball team, but he grew impatient sitting out most games on the bench and quit after half a season.

Without any real plan for his future, Dennis spent his days loafing. He'd play pool and video games and hang out with a group of kids who, like him, had nothing better to do with their time. He took on several part time jobs—like washing cars and working at a 7 Eleven—but they never lasted very long and he blew any money he earned hanging out with his friends.

After graduating from high school, Dennis still had no plans for the future. His sisters, on the other hand, were on their way to college, having been recruited by and given athletic scholarships to two notable schools: Debra to Louisiana Tech and Kim to Stephen Austin; both were named College All-Americans.

Dennis, at age 19, was working the night shift as a janitor at the Dallas-Fort Worth Airport. He swept up and mopped the airport terminal for about $6.50 an hour. One night, he stole a bunch of watches from an airport shop. He didn't steal the watches for himself, and he didn't resell them for the cash. Instead, he gave them away—to his family, friends, even people in his neighborhood whom he barely knew. He didn't want the money; he just wanted to be liked and accepted in his neighborhood.

What Dennis didn't realize was that the airport security cameras had caught him in the act. It didn't take long for the airport police to show up at his mother's house, where they arrested him and put him in jail.

Dennis was locked in a tiny cell. From time to time, angry police officers questioned him and told him he could be facing many months in jail.

Alone in his cell, thinking about having to stay locked inside for who knew how long, he started to panic. Then he began to cry.

Finally, he decided to pray. "Please God," he thought, "don't make me stay in jail. I'll never do anything like this again. I'll straighten myself up." Dennis was lucky. He cooperated with the police and helped them get all the watches back. In return, they decided to drop the charges. The experience convinced Dennis to do whatever it took never to go back to jail.

When Dennis graduated from high school, he stood 5'11". During the next year, his body had an amazing growth spurt, and he suddenly shot up to 6'8". He went back to playing basketball and found, with his increased height and strength, he was much better at it. And the more he played, the better he got.

Soon after he left jail, Dennis got another lucky break. One day, his sisters' friend Lorita Westbrook was visiting and saw Dennis playing basketball. She played basketball for Cooke County Junior College in Gainesville, Texas, about an hour away. Impressed by what she saw, Lorita arranged for him to have a tryout for the men's team at her college. Dennis still remembered his failures with high school teams; but he also remembered the promises he'd made to himself in jail, and he decided to take the risk and try out.

Basketball was an escape for both of Dennis's sisters. Debra received a scholarship at Louisiana Tech, where she was named an All-American.

The coaches at Cooke County were also very impressed by Dennis. After watching him on the court for about 15 minutes, they offered him a two-year full scholarship. Dennis happily accepted.

When the season started, though, he wondered what he'd gotten himself into. He'd never really played organized ball before; now, here he was, the starting center on a real school team in an organized competition. Once he started playing, though, he forgot about being nervous. His performance on the court was impressive; he averaged more than 17 points and 13 rebounds a game—pretty good for a complete rookie.

His performance off the court, however, was not so hot. He was failing his classes and barely making an attempt to pass. He often didn't show up for classes and didn't even take exams. Even after he'd flunked out, he could have remained in school simply by making up some of the work during the winter break, but he refused. This caused him to lose his scholarship. He seemed to assume that he would fail and it wasn't worth the trouble of trying to succeed.

Dennis was soon back in Dallas and back in the same old slump—living at home, blowing his money on video games and pool, and bumming around with a tough crowd who liked to get into all kinds of trouble

Shirley Rodman, recognizing that Dennis was flirting with disaster, gave him an ultimatum. He could get a regular job, go back to school, or go into the military. If he refused, he would have to move out of the house; she no longer would support a 19-year-old who wasn't willing to do his share. Dennis didn't like being forced to do something he didn't want to do, especially by his mother. So, without even thinking about where he could go, he left home.

Without a home and no place to live, he spent the next six months wandering the streets. Sometimes he'd sleep on the floor at a friend's house. Sometimes he'd stay awake all night, just walking around. Sometimes he'd sleep out on the streets. It was no way to live. Dennis was often exhausted and hungry. Those months on the street gave him the shock he needed to try, once again, to turn things around. He called his mother and, his voice breaking down with emotion, told her how much he wanted to come home, promising he would do something to make a change. Shirley believed him and told him to come home.

What Dennis didn't know was that some important people were looking for him. During those few months when he'd been playing on the basketball team at Cooke County college, a man named Lonn Reisman had seen Rodman play. Reisman was the assistant coach at Southeastern Oklahoma State University. Unlike Cooke County, a junior college, this was a major university that was a part of the National Association of Intercollegiate Athletics (NAIA). Reisman was really impressed by what he saw in Rodman. He knew Rodman wasn't a polished, organized player . . . yet. But he could tell that Rodman had tremendous raw talent that could be fine-tuned. He would be a substantial addition, Reisman knew, to his team.

Around the time that Shirley had agreed to let Rodman come home, Reisman called. He told Shirley he was hoping to persuade Dennis to come play for Southeastern in the fall. Thinking this was just the break Dennis needed, she told Reisman he could come to the house to meet with Dennis.

Shortly after he'd returned home, Rodman was surprised to open the door and find Lonn Reisman and Jack Hedden, the head coach at Southeastern, waiting to speak with him. Somewhat wary, Dennis sat down to hear what they had to say.

They promised Dennis he would be a valued member of the team and that he would have plenty of support to help him adjust to school and keep his grades up.

Reisman persuaded Dennis to come see the campus. As they toured the large, slick gymnasium, Reisman praised Dennis's abilities, listing what he saw as his specific strengths. "I think you can make it, Dennis," Reisman said. "I think you can be a pro." Reisman promised him that if Dennis worked hard, he'd help him become a great basketball player.

Nobody had ever really spoken this way to Dennis. His gang of friends at home had always told him not to bother even trying, that he didn't have what it takes to make it big. But here was somebody who had faith in his abilities and was willing to take a chance on him. It felt good to hear these things, and it felt great to have an idea what he could do with his life.

With a big grin on his face, he said to Reisman, "I'll do it. I want to. I want to come here."

Durant, Oklahoma, where Southeastern State is located, is 90 miles but worlds away from the Cliff Oak project where Dennis had grown up. With 4,500 students, the school was relatively large, but Dennis didn't know a soul. He was also black in a sea of white faces, and at 22, he was older than almost all the other incoming freshmen. If Dennis was going to be successful on campus, he would need a good friend to help him through.

Coaches Reisman and Hedden immediately made good on their promise to give Dennis all their support. It was still the spring, and the basketball season was months away. They found him the perfect summer job, working as a counselor at a basketball camp. He got paid to do something he loved, teaching basic basketball skills to teenage campers. He also got a friend for life.

That unlikely friend was Bryne Rich, a 13-year-old kid. Bryne was from Bokchito, a small, mostly white town in Oklahoma, where he lived with his family on a 600-acre farm. Earlier that year, his best friend Brad had been killed in a tragic hunting accident.

Desperately missing his best friend, Bryne fell into a deep depression. Plagued by terrible nightmares about the accident, he wasn't able to sleep alone in his room. He wandered around the house or his school in a daze, more like a zombie than a teenager, without any interest in doing anything he used to enjoy, including basketball. He'd planned on going to basketball camp that summer with Brad, but now he just didn't want to go any more.

Eventually his parents were able to talk Bryne into going to camp. They told him that Brad would have wanted him to go to camp as a way of remembering all the fun they used to have together. Secretly they were hoping the camp would also help Bryne get over his depression and back to his old self. Maybe he'd even make some new friends.

Bryne was assigned to the squad that Dennis coached. Often still depressed, Bryne preferred to shoot baskets by himself rather than hang out with the others. One day, his coach, Dennis, saw him shooting alone on the court and offered to give him some pointers. It soon became a part of the daily camp routine for both of them. They'd spend hours just shooting hoops and having fun on the basketball court together. Sometimes they'd also go out for a snack or play video games together. It didn't bother them that they were so different. Dennis felt like he'd suddenly found the younger brother he'd always wanted. And Bryne loved getting all this attention from an older guy who was the camp's star player.

Later that summer, Pat and James Rich couldn't help but notice how much happier Bryne was; he was laughing, joking, playing ball again. He seemed more like himself. When Bryne asked if his friend Dennis could stay overnight, they said yes. With Dennis there, Bryne was able to sleep in his old room for the first time in months.

Dennis liked staying at the Rich's house too. Pretty soon Dennis was practically living with the Riches, only spending a few nights alone back at the dorm.

Having Dennis around was strange for the Riches. They lived in a town where blacks and whites never interacted. They had never had a black person over to their home, much less practically living with them. Bryne's mother especially wasn't sure she wanted Dennis hanging around so much. Neither she nor Bryne's father had ever known a black person well and his presence made them uncomfortable. They were concerned about what their friends and neighbors would say.

Kim Rodman, Dennis's other sister, was an All-American basketball player at Stephen Austin.

Eventually they realized that skin color has nothing to do with the kind of person one is inside. They could see that Dennis was basically a good person with a lot to offer, especially to Bryne who so desperately needed a friend. Soon they opened their arms to him, although they did insist that if he wanted to stay with the family, he had to pull his share. That included doing chores around the farm, such as milking cows first thing in the morning.

Other residents were not as understanding as the Riches. When Dennis was walking around town, people would sometimes make racist comments to his face and even curse him. Dennis's first reaction was to get terribly angry; he'd want to lash out and do something violent in return. But then he'd think about Bryne, now his best friend. If he got into any kind of trouble in town, it could jeopardize his relationship with Bryne, and their friendship was just too important to Dennis to risk.

At the end of the summer, Dennis began the strenuous series of practice sessions with the team. Coaches Hedden and Reisman knew they had their work cut out for them. Sure, Dennis had raw talent. But like a diamond in the rough, it needed to be worked at and carefully honed until he became a polished professional player.

The coaches began working closely with Dennis to teach him the important skills and strategies of organized college ball. After attending the rigorous practices with the team, Dennis would often have private sessions with the coaches. They had identified Dennis's basic assets— strength, stamina, and speed. They wanted to groom him to play the post or pivot—the spot under the basket where the center stands, his back to the basket, where he can grab rebounds and relay passes to open team members or try to take a shot himself.

Dennis still had some difficulties in his school classes, but when it came to learning on the court, he was a quick study. The coaches were pleased to see how much Dennis was able to absorb in such a brief period of time. It wasn't easy for him; he had to work harder than he ever had before. But the intense training showed him how far he'd already come. The old Dennis would never have stuck it out this far. The new Dennis, though, was now committed to his team.

The first game of the season was against Southeastern State's rival, Langston University. It quickly became apparent that Dennis was ready for "big time" college ball. He was a different player than the one his coaches had first observed at the start of the training sessions. He'd absorbed all the skills and strategies they'd taught him and merged those lessons with his own natural abilities. He could pass, rebound, and score out of the post position, plus he could play tenacious defense, and his drive led him to go after loose balls other players would just let go. If the ball rebounded into the stands, Dennis dove after it.

The highlight of Dennis's debut game came in the final two minutes. Southeastern was leading by just three points with two minutes left to play. The team's strategy was to take time off the clock by passing the ball around and keeping it from their opponents at all costs. However, when Dennis got the ball, he made a move on his defender, headed to the basket, and dunked the ball, sealing the win for his team.

A year before, the Savages had had a mediocre

Rodman holds the plaque and celebrates after he and the Southeastern Oklahoma State Savages win the NAIA District 9 title in 1986.

15-13 season. With Dennis on the team, they improved to 18-9. This qualified them for the playoffs, a stepping stone to the national championships in Kansas City—something the coaches didn't even dare hope for at the start of the season.

During the first two playoff games, the Savages met two longstanding rivals. First they toppled Northeastern Oklahoma State, a team that had beaten them during the regular season. They then went on to overthrow the conference's leading team, Southwestern Oklahoma State, 81-64. Dennis's performance in both games was exceptional: 36 points and 16 rebounds in one game; 42 points and 24 rebounds in the other. Unfortunately, they lost to Phillips University, 65-59, and their hope of making it to the Nationals was quashed.

Dennis was learning that being a basketball player wasn't always going to be fun and glory. There were going to be setbacks, losses, and other unforeseen difficulties. But he now had friends offering him support, including Coaches Hedden and Reisman, and the Riches, especially Bryne. The two remained inseparable. Dennis often invited Bryne to travel with the team to away games, and Bryne soon became the Savages' water boy. People started calling him "Little Worm" because he and Dennis spent so much time together. Whenever Dennis would get down about a loss or start doubting his abilities, Bryne would say to him, "You're going to be an All-American. You're going all the way. You'll be in the NBA!" That voice of confidence got Dennis through many rough spots. Bryne believed in him, and he felt the obligation to at least try to prove he was right.

At the end of Dennis's first year at Southeastern State, one of Bryne's predictions came true: Dennis was named a First Team NAIA All-American. This was a great personal victory for him; it was rare for a player to make All-American when his team didn't make it to the Nationals, and even more rare when he was still a sophomore. There was more good news. Dennis was also named Oklahoma Intercollegiate Conference Player of the Year and District 9 Player of the Year.

After spending a summer working out with weights to add muscle and bulk, Dennis came into his junior year season faster and stronger. Right at the start of the season, he showed his stuff, dropping in 30 points and pulling down 19 rebounds. At the end of the year, he had a game in which he scored 39 points and snared 27 rebounds—a Southeastern State record. The whole team outdid their previous year's performances, claiming 20 victories in the regular season. Once again, the Savages found themselves in the conference playoffs.

As they had done the previous season, the Savages won their first two games. The only team between them and a berth in the Nationals was East Central University, to be played at the "Snake Pit," Southeastern's home court.

But 24 hours before the game, Dennis came down with a 104 fever. He was so weak he could barely stand. The coaches sat by Dennis's bedside, giving him aspirin and fluids. Little by little, the fever dropped. By game time, his temperature was normal, although he was severely weakened. Still, he insisted on playing.

The coaches rotated Dennis into the game at regular intervals, giving him plenty of breaks on the bench to rest. In limited minutes, Dennis scored 24 points and garnered 10 rebounds. More importantly, his commitment inspired his teammates. They played with motivation and pulled out a 74-68 victory, thus earning a trip to the NAIA tournament.

This was the Savages' first trip to the Nationals since 1963. They pulled a mild upset in winning their first game, 70-67, though they then lost in the second round, 60-43. Playing in the tournament was especially important for Dennis, as it brought him for the first time to the attention of NBA scouts.

After being named once again an NAIA All-American in his second year, Dennis capped his college career with his most outstanding performances. Once again, the Savages made it to the Nationals, but they far outdid their standing of the previous season. This time, they won their first three playoff games to make it to the "Final Four"—one of the four teams remaining out of the 32 at the start of the tournament. Unfortunately, a championship victory again eluded them, as poor shooting led them to lose to the University of Arkansas-Monticello, 67-61. They did, though, manage to beat St. Thomas Aquinas to take third place—pretty good for a team that until the previous year had not even made it to the Nationals in 20 years of trying.

That final game showed Dennis playing at his most spectacular. He scored 46 points, the second highest score of his career to date, and had 32 rebounds—setting a record in the NAIA for most rebounds in a national tournament. Dennis's overall season average was an amazing 17.8 rebounds, the highest in the entire NAIA. For the third straight year, he was also named NAIA All-American.

With that slew of awards and his impressive final statistics, Dennis started gaining widespread attention in the NBA, especially when he went on to be named the Most Valuable Player of the all-star postseason tournament, the Portsmouth Invitational in Virginia.

Dennis watched the NBA draft on television in the Riches' living room. When the announcer read his name and he found out he'd been drafted by the Detroit Pistons, Dennis shouted for joy and jumped in the air. The Riches flew out of their seats right alongside him, cheering and hugging him. Nobody was prouder than Bryne. He'd been right all along. The "Big Worm" was going to the NBA.

3

PISTON POWER

It was a rebound like any other—but when Rodman managed to grab this one, it caused a burst of applause from the cheering crowd, who immediately jumped to their feet. It was 1992, when Rodman was playing for the Detroit Pistons, the team he would be part of for his first seven seasons in the NBA. During a game against the Indiana Pacers, with just 59.4 seconds remaining on the overtime clock, Rodman grabbed a rebound—his 34th of the game. The rebound helped seal the Pistons' victory in the final crucial minutes of the game. But what made it so special was that with that rebound, Rodman broke the Pistons' record for the most rebounds in a single game, a record that had been set in 1972 by Bob Lanier and went unbroken for 20 years.

Danny Ainge can do nothing, as the clock has run out on the Boston Celtics during their 1985 playoff game with the Pistons. Rodman celebrates the 113-105 victory.

Rodman felt tremendous pride in this achievement, which, he told the press, represented all the hard work he'd put into his career. "I've earned all of this," he said. It also demonstrated how Dennis had managed to build a star career based on his own abilities as a rebounder.

It didn't look so certain that Rodman was destined for this kind of greatness when he first showed up in Detroit, an excited and nervous rookie. It was all so new to him. As it turned out, Dennis and the Pistons formed a perfect match. The team had many seasoned, skilled players, like Isiah Thomas, Bill Laimbeer, Adrian Dantley, and Rick Mahorn, who were willing to work with Dennis and who had a lot to teach him. And Chuck Daly, the Pistons' coach, was a patient teacher; he became almost like a father figure to Dennis, offering him much professional and personal advice.

Although Dennis got support from the team, he was disappointed to find himself spending most of his rookie year on the bench. He played in 77 of 82 games that season, but was only on the court for about 15 minutes per game. This was extremely frustrating for Dennis, who'd gone from being the star of his college team to a bench warmer. He was aching for a chance to show his stuff on the court; sitting on the bench, all of his energy bottled up without release, he felt like he'd explode. Coach Daly would tell him to be patient, assuring him that he'd get his chance.

Dennis wasn't so certain he wanted to wait. He was starting to become concerned about his future. He had made it to the NBA, but that was no guarantee he'd stay there. There were plenty of guys, he knew, who stayed on the bench for a few years and then were dropped. He hadn't worked this hard to get this far only to be dropped. He knew he had to do something to help jumpstart his career.

Dennis studied his fellow players and thought about the qualities that make for a successful NBA career. Many players, he saw, were valued for their scoring abilities, which earned them respect and widespread attention. But Dennis's strengths in college had always been his defense and rebounding. Rather than being one of dozens of average scorers, it would be much better, he realized, to be the best in the league at one skill: rebounding. And he knew, with hard work, he could transform himself into the expert rebounder he wanted to be.

During the practice sessions between his rookie and second seasons, rebounding became his primary focus. As part of practice, the team was split into squads, who would play one another in a fierce series of drills and exhibition games. Dennis started to aggressively defend against his fellow teammates on opposing squads. At first, he posed no threat to them; they were, after all, accomplished NBA veterans. But Dennis kept working at it and working at it, training himself both physically and mentally to become a rebounding dynamo. Using all that energy that had been built up from an entire season on the bench, he became a wild man on the court, grabbing rebound after rebound like his life depended on it. In a way, it did. He started to imagine that every rebound meant the difference between a star career and being dropped from the league.

He got support in these endeavors from Coach Daly. Daly knew his team didn't necessarily need another shooter, but the abilities that Dennis was now demonstrating could be a vital addition to the team. Impressed by Dennis' defensive moves, he started to put Dennis into the games for longer and longer periods of time.

At one point during Dennis' second NBA season, when his teammate Adrian Dantley injured his ankle, Daly made the decision to put Dennis in the starting lineup while Dantley was out. The Pistons went on to win 20 of the 24 games in which Dennis started, an indication of just how much rebounding could affect the outcome of a game. That Rodman's presence could influence the entire team's performance was confirmed in 1989, when Daly made Rodman a permanent part of the starting lineup as small forward to replace Mark Aguirre, who had hurt his back. With Rodman on the lineup, the team went on to a 13-game winning streak, during which the Piston defense limited the opponents to 93.5 points a game. The press hailed the Pistons as the best defensive team in the NBA and started to call Rodman the best rebounder in the league.

In his career, Rodman has since managed to transform rebounding—which had been widely considered to be mere grunt work, without the flash or hype of scoring—into an established and highly respected skill.

On the court, Rodman hustles like nobody else, chasing after rebounds most other guys would simply let go, even if it means racing across the court like a demon or diving into the second or third row of the stands. While most players will be content getting 11 or 12 rebounds a game, Rodman isn't happy unless he grabs 19 or 20. Like a marathon runner, he's trained himself to keep on going even after his body is starting to feel exhaustion or pain—he even works out after the games!—so that he can stay in the game for long periods. And, as opposing players have marveled at—and groaned about—Rodman has an uncanny ability to be right in their faces every time they get the ball. What seems like ESP is actually a combination of gut instinct and careful study of the opposition, which he uses to make split second decisions on the court.

Rodman fit in perfectly with the playing style of the Pistons in the late 1980s. The Pistons were declared the "Bad Boys" of the NBA for their rough and tough manner of play, more like wrestling or football than traditional basketball. The Bad Boy style involved being physical on the court, bumping, pushing, shoving, and even fouling, the other team. This style of play became extremely controversial. What the Pistons and their supporters called playing hard, others called playing dirty.

While controversial, the Pistons' Bad Boy moves were also successful. Piston power was at its peak in '89 and '90, when they become one of the few NBA teams to win back to back championships. Their victories in those series were particularly notable because they were largely due to their powerhouse defense, and Dennis was a crucial part of it.

Scottie Pippen thinks he can pass safely, even though seated on the floor. Little did he know Dennis Rodman was about to come flying into the picture. The Pistons won this game convincingly, 96-77, over the Bulls in the 1988 playoffs.

After having lost to the Lakers in the finals of the '88 series, the Pistons came into the following season set on making it to the finals—and taking the championship. In what would be the start of a long and fierce rivalry, the Pistons met up with the Chicago Bulls during the playoffs. It was in that series that Rodman came up against that tower of strength and muscle, Michael Jordan.

As everyone had predicted, Michael Jordan was the centerpiece of his team; when he went into overdrive, he was capable of scoring 30, 40, even 50 points a game. The entire series became a tug of war between Jordan and various members of the Piston defense trying to shut him down. The fourth game of the series was the turning point. Chicago was up two games to one in the series; if the Pistons didn't take this game to tie up the series, the chances of winning the championship were next to nil. In that same game, Rodman put on his best defensive moves. In the first half alone, he grabbed 12 rebounds and the entire Piston defense managed to keep Jordan down to just 12 points. After the third quarter, even Chicago coach Doug Collins admitted, "Rodman and Salley are killing us." Salley and Rodman alone had 11 offensive rebounds, which was four more than the entire Chicago team. At the start of the half, Daly had instructed Salley and Rodman to stay on Jordan, no matter what. "When Jordan goes to the bathroom, go with him," Daly had said. Apparently, they were following his instructions; at one point, they kept Jordan from scoring for an entire 20 minutes.

With Michael Jordan tied up and unable to hit big points, the Pistons took that game. It was a significant win because it proved to them all that Jordan could be stopped. And if he could be stopped, Chicago could be defeated.

Having triumphed over Chicago to take the Eastern Conference in the sixth game, the Pistons went on to the finals to face their old adversaries, the Los Angeles Lakers.

During the finals, Rodman was grappling with painful back spasms that forced him to sit out for long stretches. The pain didn't stop him, though, from keeping the shooting of some of the Lakers' top scorers to a minimum in Game 3, when he managed to grab 19 rebounds. The Pistons won the fourth game as well, taking the championship in a 4-0 sweep that more than made up for their defeat the previous year. It was the first championship victory in the history of the Piston franchise.

A sprained ankle prevented Rodman from playing in many of the final games the following year, when the Pistons battled the Portland Trail Blazers. Even on the injured ankle, he managed to score three points and grab nine rebounds in Game 7. But more importantly, Rodman had been instrumental in getting his team to the finals in the first place. He'd put his "game stopper" moves against Ewing and Jordan, among others, in the playoffs. The Pistons, riding that surge of momentum from their playoffs wins, took the finals.

It was one thing to be part of a team that won a championship. But back to back championships was one for the record books. Only two other teams—the Celtics and the Lakers— had been able to do it. The Pistons now could take their place among the greatest teams ever in the NBA.

Dennis Rodman (right) and his Piston teammates were greeted at the White House by Vice President Dan Quayle (left) and President George Bush after they won the NBA Championship in 1989.

What was a great year for his team was also filled with stunning personal achievements for Dennis. This was the year he was named Defensive Player of the Year for the first time. And the reason he was so deserving of that award had become evident in a game against the Houston Rockets, just before the Pistons entered the playoffs.

The game was in the final minute and the score was tied. Hakeem Olajuwon, the team's center, had hold of the ball and was making a steady drive to the basket. The court was wide open, and he had a clear and easy shot that would win his team the game. It looked to everyone like the Pistons had no chance of stopping him, but Dennis took off after him anyway. At 7'0" and 255 pounds, Olajuwon was clearly the bigger, taller, and stronger player. When he got to the basket before Rodman, even Rodman thought all was probably lost. But he'd also trained himself to fight for every ball like his career depended on it. He hurled himself after Olajuwon and, as Olajuwon jumped up with the ball preparing to dunk it, Rodman leaped from behind and flung his hand out to tap the ball. Rodman had done what seemed impossible—he blocked the shot. Everyone—including Rodman and Olajuwon—was stunned by the move. Even the crowd was silent for a few moments, trying to accept that this had actually happened. Then they burst into cheers.

Never one to hide his emotion at times like this, Dennis began to cry. "It was a moment of perfection, in line with my whole crazy life," he wrote in his book *Bad as I Wanna Be.* "I was beaten and given up for dead, but I made it back to shock the whole world."

4

A BAD BOY—
WITH STYLE

There's probably no player in the NBA as wildly loved and fiercely hated as Dennis Rodman. Rodman's hard-edged playing tactics and rebellious Bad Boy personality have earned him legions of diehard fans and a healthy share of rivals, critics, and enemies.

People tend to love or hate Rodman for the same reasons—his unpredictable spontaneity and excessive individuality. You never really know what Dennis Rodman is going to do next, on or off the court, making him tremendously exciting but also a bit dangerous. These qualities have helped him become the great rebounder he is; by always keeping his opponents guessing, he's able to gain a psychological edge that helps in his efforts to shut them down. But these bad boy maneuvers also have led to trouble. The more Rodman has walked

Scottie Pippen exacts a measure of revenge as the Chicago Bulls prevent the Pistons from three-peating as champions in 1991.

that fine line between playing hard and playing dirty, the more he's fouled out, and been penalized, fined, and suspended.

One particularly infamous Rodman skirmish came in Game Four of 1991's Eastern Conference series between the Pistons and their old rivals, the Bulls. The Pistons had succeeded in shutting down Chicago with their powerhouse Bad Boy defense twice before. But this season, the Bulls had turned the tables back on the Pistons, using the same tough style of play against them. The Bulls now easily swept the first three games of the series.

Rodman came into Game 4 extremely frustrated about those three losses and so angry he wasn't thinking clearly. In the second quarter, Bulls' forward Scottie Pippen got the ball and made a drive to the basket. Almost enraged by the Bulls' newfound successes and more determined than ever to stop them, Bill Laimbeer and Rodman were soon on Pippen. Laimbeer pushed Pippen in the chest. Rodman then shoved Pippen out of bounds, into the first row, where he hit his chin, receiving an ugly cut that would leave a scar. A flagrant foul was called on Rodman, and he was fined $5,000 by the NBA for the incident. Chicago went on to win the game and with it the Eastern Conference series, bringing them to the finals. The Pistons lost it all in an embarrassing 4-0 Bulls' winning streak.

In his defense, Rodman commented that many NBA players employ the same hard ball tactics for which he'd been penalized and criticized— they're just not caught at it. Rodman felt that as he gained a reputation, along with his Piston teammates, for being a Bad Boy, he was watched more closely by the referees, the crowds, and the

media—and therefore caught more frequently.

To many, that playoff loss in 1991 marked the beginning of the end for the great Piston Bad Boys who had once successfully won back to back championships. In the coming seasons, major changes were made that left Rodman downhearted about the state of the team. Many of the key players were traded or left. Rodman was particularly upset when Coach Daly departed following the 1992 season. Daly had been more than Rodman's coach; he'd been a mentor, friend, almost a father to Rodman.

At the same time, Rodman was going through a particularly rocky period in his personal life. He was recently divorced from Annie Bakes, a model he'd met during his rookie year. The two had had a daughter, named Alexis, who was the light of Rodman's life. The divorce was a bitter one, and Rodman was concerned about not being able to see his daughter as much as he wanted to.

The combination of the trouble with the Pistons and his personal problems made Rodman extremely depressed, which affected his performance on the court. He was late for and sometimes even missed practices and games. When he was there, he just didn't have his heart in the game and couldn't play at his best, earning him more fines and penalties. He started to make it clear to anyone who would listen that he wanted to be traded from the Pistons.

A green-haired Dennis Rodman goes in for a layup against the Los Angeles Lakers in the 1995 playoffs.

Like that one night in jail, Rodman once again thought about the track his life was on and where he wanted to be headed. Rodman realized he still wanted to do what he loved—play basketball—but also to live his life the way he chose to. In the past few years, as he'd become more successful and famous, Rodman had become aware of all the expectations everyone—the coaches, team managers, fans, press, NBA officials—had of him. They all seemed to have a particular idea of how a professional athlete should look and behave. Being an individual with his own identity was extremely important to Rodman. Rather than trying to change to fit in with someone else's image of him, he decided he would be more true to his own self-image, no matter who liked it or hated it.

Rodman asserted his "true" identity in flying, fluorescent colors—hair color that is—during a preseason exhibition event in 1993. Rodman's desire to be traded from the Pistons had been granted, and he was about to begin the season with a new team, the San Antonio Spurs. Before the official start of the season, the new team was to make its debut at an exhibition that was also the first event held in the slick and spacious new home of the Spurs, the Alamodome, making it a widely attended and covered event. When the master of ceremonies announced Rodman's name, he jogged to the center of the court and took off his hat revealing a shockingly bright yellow head of hair. The crowd roared, some booing, some cheering. "You can like me or you can hate me," he told the crowd. But on the court, he promised, "all I'm going to do is get solid."

The yellow hair was the first of a series of day-glo hair styles that are part of the flashy look that has become Rodman's trademark. In addition to technicolor hair, he has various slogans shaved onto his scalp, such as his team's logo, the peace sign, or the ribbon for AIDS awareness. He also has adorned himself with assorted tattoos, including a large portrait of his daughter.

Rodman has succeeded in creating an image of himself as a bad boy with his own unique style, more like a rock star than an athlete. One of his passions is motorcycles, and he for fun he'll rev up his Harley and zoom across the city streets. He loves to party the night away at hot clubs and dance spots with a circle of friends that includes supermodels and celebrities, including Pearl Jam's Eddie Vedder, and Madonna, whom he once dated. With his distinctive looks, Rodman has become a media sensation, appearing in scores of television spots, magazine covers, movies, and news articles. Wherever he goes, he's bombarded by autograph hounds, groupies, and packs of fans. There's a Dennis Rodman fan club and even a Dennis Rodman website where fans discuss everything from Dennis' most amazing plays to what color hair he'll choose next.

In the midst of all this fame, Rodman has made certain not to forget his roots. Whenever he's back in Dallas, he makes it a point to return to the Oak Cliff project. This helps remind him of the path his life could have taken were it not for all his hard work. His months on the street also make him particularly sympathetic to the homeless; he's been known to give up to $1,000 to homeless people he sees on the street. He also likes to pass out free tickets to people who can't afford to come to his games.

Coach Bob Hill watches carefully as Rodman rebounds a Houston miss in front of Sam Cassell. The Rockets beat the Spurs, and team officials felt that Rodman proved more of a distraction than a help during the playoffs.

Rodman's flashy image and highly publicized antics make him a particularly popular attraction at basketball games. Even when Rodman's team is playing in other cities, crowds flock to get a look at him and see what unexpected things he'll do on the court. During Rodman's first year on the Spurs, attendance at their games was second in the entire NBA, and the television ratings soared.

While on the Spurs, Rodman's rebounding was also at its finest. He led the NBA in rebounding both years he was on the Spurs which, combined with the two years he won that title on the Pistons, made him a four-time leader. In his second year, Rodman played in 49 games and the Spurs won 43 of them, the best record that year in the NBA. Rodman also helped bring the Spurs to the Western Conference finals for the first time.

While Rodman's athletic abilities may have been at their best, his appearance and actions did not sit so well with the team management, coaches, and other players. They had a certain idea about the way the game should be played and the image an NBA player should convey. They also had certain set rules for the team's conduct they insisted be followed. But Rodman didn't always want to play by their rules and he also didn't always agree with their coaching decisions. This created tension between Rodman and the Spurs' management that eventually resulted in open conflict.

One incident came during the 1994 playoffs, when the Spurs were playing the Utah Jazz. In the second game of the series, Rodman stuck his hip out, sending point guard John Stockton flying into the air. The NBA fined Dennis $10,000 and suspended him from the next game, the third in the series, which the Spurs lost, 105-72.

Rodman was again doing what he always did—playing Bad Boy hard ball—but getting caught and heavily penalized for it. Rodman felt that his Bad Boy reputation made him more closely watched and penalized than his fellow players. The Spurs' management, though, felt that Rodman was jeopardizing the team.

During the playoff series the following year, the tension between Rodman and the Spurs'

Rodman is supposed to be ready to sub in for the Spurs—but he's not wearing his sneakers. Rodman was protesting being held out of the starting lineup after he showed up late for practice.

management reached a peak. It was during the Western Conference Semifinals series against the Lakers. In Game 3, Rodman came off the court during a time out and took his shoes off. This was something Rodman said he always did during games to air his feet. But the management thought it was an affront to them and the team. It was made worse when Rodman didn't join the team huddle, but sat leaning back on sidelines with his shoes off. Bob Hill, the Spurs' coach, and Gregg Popovich, the Spurs' manager, kept him out of the rest of the game and decided to suspend him from Game 4 for insubordination. The Spurs won Game 4 without him. The management then decided not to let him start in Game 5, which the Spurs also won to take the L.A. series.

Winning without Rodman in those two games led the Spurs to think they didn't necessarily need him on the team. But the team wound up losing in the Western Conference finals to the Houston Rockets. Many blamed Rodman for the loss, claiming that he was a distraction for the players and that he wasn't giving the Spurs his all. Rodman felt they were again making him the target, blaming him rather than looking at other weak spots on the team.

It was clear to everyone that things were just not going to work out between Rodman and the Spurs. Rodman wanted to be off the team, and the Spurs wanted to be rid of him. So, before the 1995-1996 season, they traded him to the Chicago Bulls. A few months later, the Bulls were being called the Greatest Team in the NBA. Ever.

5

RODMAN ON THE REBOUND

Whenthe Worm came to Chicago, he stopped traffic—literally. In March 1996, a men's clothing warehouse located alongside the Kennedy Expressway erected a 32-foot-high mural of Rodman in all his technicolor and tattooed splendor. Traffic along the busy expressway slowed to a standstill as gawkers slowed their vehicles and craned their necks for a better look; some drivers even stopped their cars to get out and take photographs. After two weeks of heavy-duty traffic delays, the mural was painted over and traffic returned to normal.

It may have been possible to whitewash over the painting, but Rodman the man had clearly made a permanent impression on Chicago. At Bulls' games, packs of Rodman fans—the "Rodmaniacs" as they were dubbed—crowded the stands waving signs in praise of their beloved

This giant billboard of Rodman didn't last long—it came down soon after being erected. Traffic had snarled as drivers slowed to take a good look at it.

Worm. That reception is all the more remarkable when you consider that, back when he'd been on the Pistons, Chicago considered Rodman on par with Freddy Krueger for his Bad Boy defensive maneuvers.

When the Bulls first considered taking on Rodman before the start of the season, there was much speculation as to whether this was a wise decision. Everyone wondered if it was possible to tame the wild Worm. Would he behave? Or would he be up to his explosive antics that had gotten him into so much trouble in San Antonio?

To Bulls coach Phil Jackson and general manager Jerry Krause, signing on Rodman was a risk well worth taking. They'd spent several weeks carefully considering the trade and held intensive, one-on-one sessions with Rodman himself. They were convinced that Rodman wanted to play basketball far more than to make trouble. They also had practical motives. Rodman filled a glaring hole in their front line—the power forward. If they hoped to overcome some of the NBA's powerhouse teams that season—including the Orlando Magic, the team that had flushed them out of the Eastern Conference series in the second round in 1995—they'd need a power forward with Rodman's guts and drive.

Rodman arrived at his first game of the season with the Bulls' logo shaved into his fire-engine red hair to show support for his new team. He didn't get the chance to make his mark on the team, though, until several weeks later, as a calf injury kept him out of 12 games early in the season. Returning to face the New York Knicks, he asserted his presence and showed the kind of difference his rebounding could make

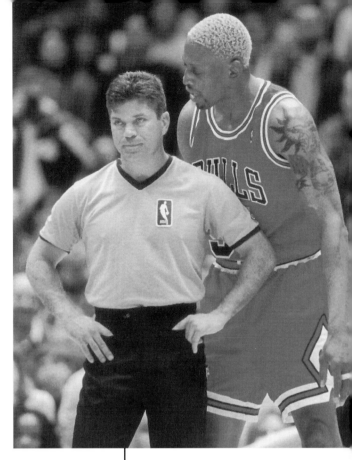

to the team. The Bulls had a poor first half, where even Jordan was not scoring up to par. But then out came Rodman. Playing, as teammate Michael Jordan would later say, "like a rebounding fool," Rodman jumped and dove after balls, shaking his hands in the air after successful plays like a sports fan doing the wave. He also succeeded in hitting a free throw that had been passed off to him by Jordan that brought the Bulls to within one point of the win by the end of the third quarter.

His enthusiasm energized the entire team, including Jordan, who came alive in the second half, shooting stronger and bringing the Bulls into the lead. At one point, Jordan approached Rodman as he prepared to take his foul shots and the two embraced. The crowd went wild; they could see this one-of-a-kind team coming together, beginning to do all they were capable of. Rodman finished the game with 20 rebounds, and the Bulls won 101-94.

An incident later in the season, though, once again put Rodman at the center of controversy. In a game against the New Jersey Nets, a referee called two technical fouls on Rodman which, according to NBA regulations, means automatic ejection from the game. An angry Rodman stalked over to the referee and proceeded to ram his head into the referee's skull. For the head butting, the NBA gave Rodman the third-stiffest penalty possible, suspending him for six games without pay and fining him $20,000.

Rodman has gotten into repeated difficulty with referees. Here he argues with Ted Bernhardt after having been ejected during the first quarter of a 1996 game against the New Jersey Nets. Rodman then bumped the ref, knocked over a water cooler, and shouted obscenities as he left the court.

The suspension came at a particularly troublesome time for the Bulls. They'd been having a fantastic season so far and it looked like they might become the first NBA team to win 70 games in a single season. But then Scottie Pippen was forced out with a back injury, and Rodman was suspended. Rodman's critics were quick to say, "I told you so," claiming the incident showed there was no taming the Worm and he'd only keep sabotaging his team's chances of success.

Rodman returned from his suspension determined to show his team that he would not disappoint them in the future. In his first game back, he grabbed 13 rebounds, more than anyone else on the Bulls, and scored eight points. In future games, he maintained a 14.9 rebound average that made him the top rebounder in the NBA for the fifth year in a row.

And on April 16, the entire team went into the record books. Beating Milwaukee 86-80, the Bulls' sealed their 70th victory of the season. Surpassing the record set in 1972 by the Los Angeles Lakers (who had won 69 games), the Bulls became the team with the most wins in a single season. The Bulls then went on to top the record, finishing the season with an astonishing 72 wins and 10 losses.

But Rodman's greatest moments of personal glory came in that year's playoffs and finals, when he proved his worth to the Bulls and showed the world all the Worm could do.

From the start of the season, the Bulls had been eagerly waiting for the chance to take on the Orlando Magic and make up for their loss in the previous year's playoffs. From the start of the series, it was apparent that the Bulls would dominate.

Chicago won the first game of the series, 121-83, and they did it without having to rely solely on Jordan's scoring (Jordan scored 21 points, still an impressive number but not in his usual high range). Running all over the court like there was fire in his veins, Rodman managed to put himself wherever the ball was. In the first quarter, he alone claimed more rebounds than the entire opposing team; he finished the game with a total of 21 rebounds. He also scored 13 points, a season high for him. And, never one to let his personal discomfort get in the way of his game, he did it all with a stomach virus.

For Rodman, who always looks forward to going up against the other team's powerhouse players, the game's best moments came in his guarding Shaquille O'Neal, the 7'1", 300-pound Magic center. O'Neal, one of the strongest players in the league, had led the NBA in scoring during the previous season with a 29.3 point per game average. But Rodman was able to contain him. In the third quarter, the Bulls were leading, 63-51, close enough that the game could have gone either way, especially if O'Neal managed to get to the basket. Jackson sent Rodman out to guard O'Neal and, in the final five minutes of the quarter, Rodman limited Shaq to just one field goal. With Rodman on top of him, O'Neal missed four shots and gave up the ball twice. The Bulls finished the quarter with 18 more points to the Magic's 5, providing them with a strong enough lead to insure a victory.

The Bulls went on to decimate the Magic, sweeping the entire series, 4 games to 0.

If Rodman was a dynamo in the playoffs, he became a tornado in the finals series against the Seattle SuperSonics. A strong presence through-

Some have said that Rod-man's tattoos and piercings show a hatred for the black-ness of his skin. True or not, it didn't help Frank Brickow-ski or the Seattle SuperSonics during the 1996 Finals.

out the series, Rodman's talents were at a peak in Game 2. The Sonics were expecting the most trouble from Jordan and geared their defensive strategy to stopping him; the strategy worked, somewhat, in that Jordan did not dominate the game (he did score 29 points, but the Sonics kept him to just 9 of 22 shots from the field). But they hadn't been prepared for the techni-colored, tattooed demon. Rodman grabbed a total of 20 rebounds, 11 of which were offensive rebounds, tying the record for most offensive rebounds in a game. Nine of those offensive rebounds came in the second half of the game, making them particularly important as the Son-ics had managed to close an 18-point gap between the teams.

Rodman was the man of the moment in the climactic final seconds of the game. With only

8.9 seconds on the clock, Chicago led 91 to 88, hardly enough of a lead to guarantee a win. At that moment, Scottie Pippen was fouled; if he successfully made his free throws, the Chicago lead would be large enough to guarantee a win. But Pippen's second shot touched the rim and then bounced back. As the ball flew back onto the court, Rodman zipped out to make a grab for it, fighting through a pack of other players all with the same idea. He and Sam Perkins flew on the loose ball at the same time.

With 6.9 seconds left, Rodman's hustle play set up a crucial jump ball. The air in the arena became thick with anticipation and excitement. The entire game came down to this moment. If the Sonics grabbed the jump ball, they had the opportunity to set up a three pointer that would tie the game. The referee threw up the ball, and the players jumped up after it. The two teams made a mad scramble for the ball, and Pippen managed to work his way to it. He passed it to Rodman but in the confused dash for the ball Rodman was fouled.

Rodman now found himself in an unusual but imperative position. While he excels at rebounding, no one ever expects much from him when it comes to shooting. Now, he was in a position to earn the points his team needed to insure a win in a finals game. Rodman studied the basket for a moment and then made his first shot. The ball missed the basket. With a deep breath and intense concentration, he prepared his second shot. With a light touch, he tossed the ball toward the basket; it soared through the air and gracefully hit the basket. He'd made the shot. The crowd exploded in cheers. Rodman had sealed his team's win, 92-88.

Dennis Rodman, Scottie Pippen, Coach Phil Jackson, and Michael Jordan sit with their NBA trophies at their feet during the championship celebration in Chicago's Grant Park in 1996.

After the Bulls won the first three games of the finals, the Sonics came back to win the next two. But when play returned to Chicago, back on the Bulls' home turf, they again showed the stuff that championship teams are made of, once more rallying their relentless team defense. During the final game, Rodman earned 19 rebounds; he also got five points at a crucial moment in the third quarter when the Bulls turned a 57-47 lead into a 64-47, shattering the Sonics' hopes of pulling ahead. The Bulls took the finals, four games to two. And Rodman was able to bring home his third championship ring.

Rodman could take particular personal pride in this victory. Pictures of a grinning Rodman, his hands raised in triumph on the court, were all over the press, where he received widespread praise for his instrumental role in the series. His performance—and his career—had shown how rebounding can make all the difference in a game, even in a championship.

In the next season, Rodman averaged 16

rebounds per game to lead the league. With the NBA leaders in both rebounding and scoring— Michael Jordan again led the league in that category—the Bulls again bulldozed their way through the Central Division, winning the division title with a 69-13 record.

In the playoffs, the Bulls easily defeated their first three opponents, Washington, Atlanta, and Miami. In the finals, Chicago overcame a strong Utah Jazz team to win its second straight NBA title, four games to two.

Dennis again helped the Bulls to the title. Playing in all 19 games, he led the team in rebounding and averaged 4.2 points per game during the playoffs. And with the victory over Utah, he became the first player in the history of the NBA to win back-to-back championships with two different teams—first with the Pistons in 1988-89 and 1989-90, and now with the Bulls.

In 1998 Rodman again led the league in rebounding as the Bulls won the NBA Central Division with a 62-20 record. Despite some difficulty from an experienced Indiana Pacers team in the playoff semifinals, the Bulls again reached the NBA finals, once again facing the Jazz. And yet again, the Bulls were victorious, as Rodman helped them win in six games. The championship ring he earned was his fifth.

For years, kids playing basketball have spent hours honing their shooting skills, dreaming of one day earning that game-winning basket and earning all the glory of a Magic Johnson or a Michael Jordan. Now, thanks to Dennis Rodman, you just might want to work on ways to "worm" around the court, dreaming of diving for those hard to reach rebounds that also earn applause and cheers.

DENNIS RODMAN
A CHRONOLOGY

1961   Dennis Rodman is born on May 31 to Shirley and Philander Rodman

1964   Dennis moves with his mother and two sisters to the Oak Cliff Projects in Dallas

1980   While working as a janitor in the Dallas Ft. Worth airport, Dennis is arrested for stealing some watches. After spending a night in jail, he swears to turn his life around

1982   After a friend of his sisters arranged a tryout for him, Dennis plays for Cooke County Junior College for one semester. Failing grades force him to give up his scholarship and drop out of school

1983   After several months living on the streets, Dennis once again vows to make a change in his life. Coaches Hedden and Reisman, who had watched him play at Cooke County, recruit him to play for Southeastern Oklahoma State. At basketball camp, he befriends Bryne Rich, who would become his best friend

1986   Dennis leads the Savages to a "Final Four" appearance in the NAIA National tournament; Dennis is named NAIA All-American three years in a row; After being named MVP of the Virginia Invitational post-season tournament, Dennis is drafted by the Detroit Pistons

1989   After having lost the NBA finals to the Lakers during the previous season, Detroit sweeps the series, 4-0. This is the first championship victory in Piston history

1990   The Pistons beat the Portland Trail Blazers to become one of three teams to win back-to-back NBA championships; Rodman is named Defensive Player of the year

1991   The Pistons lose to the Chicago Bulls in the playoffs; Rodman is again named Defensive Player of the Year

1992   Rodman leads the NBA in rebounding with an average of 18.7, the highest in the NBA in 20 years; he also breaks the Pistons' record for most rebounds in a single game

1994   Rodman is traded to the San Antonio Spurs; in the pre-season opening exhibition game, Rodman shows up with his hair dyed platinum blonde and his ever-changing, brightly colored hair becomes a Dennis Rodman trade mark

1995   Out of 49 games in which Rodman played, the Spurs win 43 and end up with the best record in the NBA. The Spurs make it to the Western Conference finals, but Rodman is suspended for taking his shoes off during a team huddle; the Spurs lose the Conference finals to the Houston Rockets, and Rodman is traded to the Chicago Bulls

1996   Rodman is once again at the center of controversy when he is fined and suspended for head butting a referee; Chicago becomes the first team ever to win 70 games; Rodman earns his third championship ring as the Bulls defeat Seattle in the Finals

1997   Dennis becomes the first player in NBA history to win back-to-back championships with two different teams as the Bulls repeat as league champions

1998   Dennis helps the Chicago Bulls win the championship by beating out the Utah Jazz, earning his fifth championship ring

STATISTICS

DENNIS RODMAN

Regular Season

Season	Team	G	FGM	FGA	Pct	FTM	FTA	Pct	REB	AST	PTS	AVG
1986-87	Det	77	312	391	.545	74	126	.587	332	56	500	6.5
1987-88	Det	82	398	709	.581	152	294	.535	715	110	953	11.6
1988-89	Det	82	316	531	.595	97	155	.626	772	99	735	9.0
1989-90	Det	82	288	496	.581	142	217	.654	792	72	719	8.8
1990-91	Det	82	276	580	.493	111	176	.631	1026	85	669	8.2
1991-92	Det	82	342	635	.539	84	140	.600	**1530**	191	800	9.8
1992-93	Det	62	183	429	.427	87	163	.534	**1132**	102	468	7.5
1993-94	SA	79	158	292	.534	53	102	.520	**1367**	184	370	4.7
1994-95	SA	49	137	240	.571	76	111	.676	823	97	349	7.1
1995-96	Chi	64	146	304	.480	56	106	.528	952	160	351	6.5
1996-97	Chi	55	128	286	.448	50	88	.568	883	170	311	5.7
1997-98	Chi	80	155	360	.431	61	111	.550	**1200**	232	375	4.7
TOTALS		876	2839	5253	.540	1043	1789	.583	11,524	1558	6600	7.5

Playoffs

Season	Team	G	FGM	FGA	Pct	FTM	FTA	Pct	REB	AST	PTS	AVG
1986-87	Det	15	40	74	.541	18	32	.563	71	3	98	6.5
1987-88	Det	23	71	136	.522	22	54	.407	136	21	164	7.1
1988-89	Det	17	37	70	.529	24	35	.686	170	16	98	5.8
1989-90	Det	19	54	95	.568	18	35	.514	161	17	126	6.6
1990-91	Det	15	41	91	.451	10	24	.417	177	14	94	6.3
1991-92	Det	5	16	27	.593	4	8	.500	51	9	36	7.2
1993-94	SA	3	12	24	.500	1	6	.167	48	2	25	8.3
1994-95	SA	14	52	96	.542	20	35	.571	207	18	124	8.9
1995-96	Chi	18	50	103	.485	35	59	.593	247	37	135	7.5
1996-97	Chi	19	30	81	.370	15	26	.577	160	26	79	4.2
1997-98	Chi	21	39	105	.371	23	38	.605	247	42	102	4.9
Totals		169	442	902	.490	190	352	.540	1675	205	1081	6.4

G	games		FTA	free throws attempted
FGM	field goals made		REB	rebounds
FGA	field goals attempted		AST	assists
Pct	percent		PTS	points
FTM	free throws made		AVG	average

bold indicates league leading figures

SUGGESTIONS FOR FURTHER READING

Rodman, Dennis, with Tim Keown. *Bad As I Wanna Be.* New York: Delacorte Press, 1996.

Rodman, Dennis, Pat Rich, and Alan Steinberg. *Rebound: The Dennis Rodman Story.* New York: Crown Publishers, 1994.

Stauth, Cameron. *The Franchise: Building a Winner with the World Champion Detroit Pistons, Basketball's Bad Boys.* New York: William Morrow, 1990.

ABOUT THE AUTHOR

A college instructor and professional writer, Steven Frank is the author of *Magic Johnson, The Allisons, A+ Term Papers, The Road to College,* and *The Everything Study Book.* He lives in New York City.

INDEX

PHOTO CREDITS
AP/Wide World Photos: 2, 11, 12, 14, 35, 40, 43, 46, 48, 50, 53, 56, 58; Detroit Free Press: 8; courtesy Louisiana Tech: 18; courtesy Stephen Austin Sports: 23; UPI/Bettmann: 30; George Bush Presidential Library: 38.